A L♥VEBIRD NAMED LUCY

by
Jaklen Alkyan

A Lovebird Named Lucy
Copyright © 2020 by Jaklen Alkyan
All rights reserved.

Published 2020
United States of America
ISBN 978-0-578-67005-8
First Edition

Cover, layout and illustration
by Victoria Caro Johnson

To learn more about Lucy visit
www.alovebirdnamedlucy.com

With every happiness that passes,
something beautiful remains; the
memories that will last for a lifetime.
This book is dedicated to my lovebird, Lucy.
The story of how I lost and found her.
Spread your wings my beautiful lovebird
and soar into the sky.

Lucy was overjoyed when a beautiful
young girl stopped in front of the cage.
Lucy hopped around and flapped her
wings excitedly, singing a joyful song. The
girl said, "My name is Audrey. Can I be
your mommy? Will you be my lovebird?"

She was so warm and friendly that
Lucy tweeted, "Yes I want to come home
with you!"

Lucy was a lovebird with beautiful white, gray and aqua-blue feathers. She lived in California with other birds like her. They were young and without a home, like Lucy, who was only three months old. Their mommies and daddies had gone, leaving the little birds to find new, loving homes.

Lucy sat in a cage at a bird show watching people walk by, wondering if someone would take her home. She heard people say, "Hello!" and "Aren't you cute?" but then walk away.

Lucy's dream was to find a mommy who would love her and take good care of her. She imagined living in a beautiful home with a mommy who would let her fly freely through the house and into the backyard. She imagined singing sweet songs all day and into the night.

Audrey brought Lucy to her new home. She hopped around the floor and flew around the rooms. There were big rooms and small rooms. Outside were tall trees and bright green grass.

"I love my new home!" Lucy tweeted.

Audrey fed Lucy delicious bread, eggs and chicken. It was so yummy Lucy would get excited and fly into the air with food in her beak, making a mess.

"Sorry!" Lucy tweeted.
"It's ok, my little lovebird," Audrey giggled.

Lucy followed Audrey everywhere.
Whenever Audrey was doing her chores,
Lucy would be right by her side.

"Can I help?" she would tweet.
Audrey would kiss Lucy and Lucy would
kiss her back.

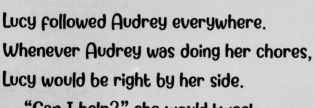

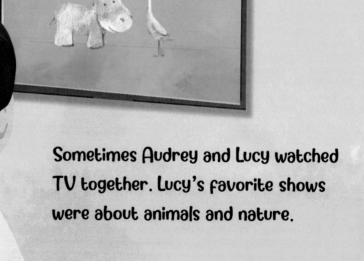

Sometimes Audrey and Lucy watched
TV together. Lucy's favorite shows
were about animals and nature.

Audrey invited her friends and family over to meet Lucy. She sat on the edge of a table and sang for them. Everyone clapped and exclaimed, "Lucy is a beautiful lovebird!"

One day, Audrey went to visit her grandparents and brought Lucy with her. Lucy sat in her cage outside enjoying the fresh air and bright sunshine. She enjoyed it so much that she pushed open the door to her cage and flew away!

She flew high into the sky wishing her mommy could see her. She flew over big houses, over rolling hills, down to a tree where she saw other birds. She chirped at them and they chirped back.

"Don't you have a flock?" the other birds asked.

"No, I have a mommy," said Lucy. "I live in a house."

The other birds that lived in the wild didn't know what a house was. They imagined it must be delightful from what Lucy told them.

"I can sing for my mommy's friends and eat bread, eggs and chicken. I get to listen to music too!"

Lucy said goodbye to her new friends and flew away. She flew and flew until she was tired. All this time she had no idea that her mommy was looking for her and was very worried.

Lucy landed on a big roof that overlooked a valley. The sun was setting and she realized that her mommy was nowhere in sight. She flew east and west, landing on trees, bushes and finally on the roof of a big house to see if her mommy was nearby.

Meanwhile, Audrey was frantic looking for her sweet Lucy. She walked the streets calling out her name, hoping Lucy would hear her and fly back to her. She asked her friends and family to help her put signs up around the neighborhood asking for help to find her little bird.

14

Lucy grew tired and scared as she realized she was lost. When the sun set, she found a warm spot to rest for the night. She would start searching for her home again in the morning.

When Lucy woke up, she thought about how much she missed her mommy and where she should start looking for her.

As she sat thinking, she heard a man call out her name.

"Luuuucy? Where are you, Lucy?"

Lucy was afraid. She didn't know this man or if the man would hurt her. He started to climb up on the roof so Lucy swooped down and bit him!

"Ouch!" the man said, "I'm trying to help you, little bird."

Lucy flapped her wings and tweeted, "I'm sorry mister. I didn't know you were trying to help. I hope you're okay!"

"I'm okay," said the man. "My name is John and that's my wife Maggie down there. We want to help you."

OUCH!

Lucy tweeted again. She told John she had lost her mommy and couldn't find her way home. John tried to pick her up but Lucy hopped away and flew into the sky, over the neighborhood, while John and Maggie called out, "Come back, little bird! We want to help you!"

Lucy didn't know what to do. She was scared and alone and wanted to go home. She flew high into the sky, sailing through clouds and flapping her wings hard, searching for her home.

"Is that my home over there?" she wondered. She flew closer, but no, it wasn't her home.

"Is that my home down by the water?" she asked herself. She flew closer, but no, it wasn't her home, it was just a big rock.

Lucy flew all day looking for her home. She flew to the mountains and out to the sea, but still couldn't find her mommy. She searched another day until she landed by a little cottage with bright flowers and soon fell fast asleep. She was weak and tired and needed to rest.

When Lucy woke up, she saw John again who reached out his hands and said, "Don't worry, little one. We're going to find you a loving home."

"But I have a home!" Lucy tweeted. "My mommy Audrey is my home!"

John gently picked up Lucy who decided to trust him. He wanted to bring her to a doctor to make sure she was okay and to get help in finding her a home.

At the doctor's office, the doctor told Lucy, "You're a very healthy little bird. Someone was taking good care of you. We'll find you a good home."

"But I have a home!" Lucy tweeted. She hoped with all her might that her mommy would find her.

It was not her mommy but another girl who found Lucy at the doctor's. Her name was Rachel and she was pretty and sweet, just like her mommy, Audrey. She told Lucy she would give her a new home.

"Come along, little bird," said Rachel warmly.

In Rachel's home Lucy was fed bread
and bird seed. She missed her eggs
and chicken. Lucy liked Rachel and
Rachel took good care of her, but
she still wished that Audrey would
find her.

Meanwhile, Audrey, with
friends and family by her side,
searched high and low for Lucy.
Everyone hoped that Lucy was safe
and would find her way home.

LUCY!

One bright morning Lucy woke up and heard Rachel asking someone, "Is this your lovebird?"

Then Lucy heard a familiar voice. When she looked up she saw her mommy waving at her! With the help of friends, family and a caring community, Audrey was able to find her Lucy.

Lucy flapped her wings excitedly and flew across the room, landing on Audrey's shoulder.

"Oh you gave me a scare!" Audrey cried. "I'm so glad I found you, my sweet Lucy!"

It had been six days since Audrey saw Lucy, almost an entire week!

"I missed you so much!" Lucy tweeted.

Audrey brought Lucy home and fed her delicious food. Lucy felt loved and safe.

Together again, Lucy and Audrey snuggled, watched their favorite TV shows and sang their favorite songs. Lucy was home for good and promised her mommy she would never fly away again.

To learn more about Lucy visit
www.alovebirdnamedlucy.com

ABOUT THE AUTHOR

Jaklen Alkyan is an Assyrian woman born in Iran. In 1989 she left Iran as a refugee and resided in Germany before making the United States her home in 1993.

Jaklen obtained a Bachelor of Arts degree in Psychology from California State University, Stanislaus, and a Master's degree in Education from University of Phoenix.

She is a well-traveled Human Resources Executive. Her unconditional love for children and animals led Jaklen to her passion for writing.

Jaklen is an aspiring author with A Lovebird Named Lucy as her literary debut. She lives in Los Angeles, California.

Made in the USA
Monee, IL
21 August 2020